This book belongs to:

· · · · · · · · · · · · · · · · · · · ·

THE FOREVER STREET FAIRIES: NOGO AND HIS MUFFLING MAGIC

by Hiawyn Oram and Mary Rees

British Library Cataloguing in Publication Data

A catalogue record of this book is available from

the British Library.

ISBN 0 340 84140 0

First edition published 2003

10 9 8 7 6 5 4 3 2 1

Published by Hodder Children's Books
a division of Hodder Headline Limited
338 Euston Road London NW1 3BH

Printed in Hong Kong

THE Forever Street Fairies

Nogo and his Muffling Magic

Written by

Hiawyn Oram

Illustrated by

Mary Rees

h

*Hodder
Children's
Books*

A division of Hodder Headline Limited

Contents
· · · · · · · · · ·

Chapter One

Rainbow Makes A Big Mistake

It was spring
and the fairies were getting ready
for their Bluebell Time Concert.

Rainbow was telling everyone
what to do.

"Build the stage higher, Elfie."
"Hang the curtain straighter,
Luckyday."
"Stop giggling, Pea and Pod!"

She was in such a bossy mood
she even dared order Cyclone about.
"Stop spying on us, White Beast,
or I'll make sure Miss Wand
shuts you in the kitchen!"

And then, as Cyclone slunk deeper
into the bluebells,
she made her big mistake.
She told Nogo what to do.

"That machine is making
such a noise I can't think.
Muffle it with your Magic
Muffling Powder this minute!"
And off she flew to deliver
Miss Wand's invitation
to the concert.

Chapter Two

Nogo Throws A Tantrum

Nogo's face turned red.

He beat his fairy feet

on the ground

and punched the air

with his tiny fairy fists.

Fingers and Speedwell
tried to calm him.
"But she told me what to do,"
he sobbed. "Nobody tells me what
to do! I know what to do without
being told!"
"She didn't mean it,"
soothed Speedwell.
"She has a lot to think about."
"And so have I!" said Nogo.
And he stamped off home,
as hard as a fairy can stamp,
which isn't very hard at all.

Chapter Three

Whiskers At The Window

Back home, Nogo played

his pot and pan drums

then went to sort out

his Interesting Twigs and

Acorn Cups.

This always made him feel better.

Soon he was back to his

best self again...

happy, cheeky and very mischievous.

So when he looked up
and saw a large eye
at the window
and two long whiskers,
he wasn't afraid.
He wasn't even alarmed.

"Ho, ho, White Beast,"
he chuckled.
"You don't scare
me...!" And he flew
up on to one
of the whiskers,

walked it like
a tightrope,
dropped down
and swung on it!

But he wasn't quite
fast enough.
Cyclone's paw
sneaked up and
swiped him on to
the grass outside.

Now Nogo thought
he was in BIG trouble.
But Cyclone only smiled slyly.
"You and me, Nogo," he hissed,
"we've got some talking to do.
About that fairy
who tells us what to do."

Chapter Four

The White Beast's Wicked Plan

Nogo tried to sit up.

Cyclone kept him down.

"Well? You want to hear my plan?"

"Maybe…" said Nogo.

"Not maybe," Cyclone hissed,
stroking a whisker.
"All right," said Nogo.
"Tell me it."

Cyclone checked
no one was listening
and whispered his plan.

It was a wicked plan.

And deep down Nogo knew it.

But he felt so mischievous

he decided to think of it

as all just good fun.

So when Cyclone finished

he leapt up and cried,

"You're right, White Beast!

She should be taught a lesson.

And who better to teach her

than me?"

Chapter Five

Nogo Goes Sprinkling Mad

No one saw Nogo
until just before the concert.
He arrived in the woods
with a naughty grin
and his Sprinkler of Magic
Muffling Powder.

"Hello Speedwell!" he called.
"Hello Nogo," said Speedwell
carefully. "Now, I wonder...
would you be kind enough
to help me set out the food
for after the concert?"
"Of course I will," chuckled Nogo.
"As you asked so nicely.

And if I can have a cake.

I'm starving!

And after I've done

what I have to do first."

"Go on then," said Speedwell.

Nogo helped himself

to a fairy cake. "I'll be back

in a moment," he said.

Carrying the cake
he hurried over to the stage
where Rainbow was still bossing
everyone around.
"Hello all," he said.
"Hello Rainbow."
Rainbow stopped.
"What are you doing
with that cake, Nogo?
It's not for now.
Put it back at once."

17

"WHAT did you say?" said Nogo.

Fingers nudged Rainbow.

"Don't tell him what to do,

remember."

But Rainbow still wasn't

listening to anyone.

"I said put the cake back.

Then help Bristle sweep the stage."

In a flash Nogo was waving
his Sprinkler at Rainbow.
For a moment
she couldn't be seen
for a cloud of
Magic Muffling
Powder.

Then she opened
her mouth to speak
but not a sound
came out.
The fairies gasped.
"Nogo!" cried
Speedwell rushing up.
"What have
you done?"

"Muffled her, of course!"
Nogo danced about with delight.
"So now she CAN'T tell me
what to do.
She can't tell ANYONE what to do.
And about time too!"

"But what about the concert?"
exploded Speedwell.
"Rainbow is singing four songs and
making all the announcements.
Un-muffle her at once!"

"AND SILENCE TO YOU TOO!"
cried Nogo, "for telling me
what to do!"
And, as if his magic
had gone to his head,
he sprinkled Speedwell.
And when Elfie
told him to stop it,
he sprinkled HIM.

And when Bristle rushed up
and told him to stop it,
he sprinkled HIM...
and STILL chuckling,
he flew up into a tree.

Chapter Six

Pea And Pod Go Fishing

"He's gone sprinkling mad!"
said Fingers.
"And if we're not careful
we'll ALL be muffled,
and we'll have to cancel
the concert!"

"We can't do that,"
said Mr Snip Snap.
"Miss Wand may be coming."
"Well, what ARE we going to do?"
said Luckyday.

Pea and Pod picked up
their magic fishing rods.
"We could go... fishing!
For his Good Manners!"
"Try it!" cried Fingers.

So the Peaspods stood on a log.
They cast their magic fishing lines
into the magic blue and sang,
"Magic rods and magic lines,
This is the magic we would hatch...
For all good manners that are lost
Those good manners you must catch!"

For a moment nothing
happened.
Then...
WHOOSH!
...the lines
whipped
into the air,

looped
and
curled,

and dropped two little blue sacks
tied with ivy
at the Peaspods' feet.

26

"Nogo," Fingers called.

"The Peaspods have something
for you!"

"It had better be something good!"
Nogo called back.

"It's very good," said Fingers.

So Nogo flew down.

He never could resist a gift.

He examined the sacks.

"Which one first? This one I think!"
He pulled the ivy cord
and peered inside.

At once his naughty grin vanished
and a big kindly smile spread
from ear to ear.
"My Manners!" he beamed.
"My beautiful Good Manners!
I quite forgot them!

But now they're back
I want to say...
I was wrong to muffle you,
Rainbow, and you, Speedwell
and Elfie and Bristle.
I was wrong to listen to
Cyclone's plan..."

"*Cyclone's plan?*"

exploded Fingers.

"Muffling us was the

White Beast's idea?"

"Oh yes," said Nogo sweetly.

"He won't have Rainbow telling

him what to do either.

But the thing is...

I carried out his plan.

How can I make it up to you?"

"By un-muffling them, of course!"
cried Luckyday.
"And fast," cried Fingers.
"Look the hedgehogs are arriving
for the concert!"

Nogo's smile vanished.

He went white as a snowdrop.

"But," he gasped, "my magic

takes its own time to wear off.

I DON'T KNOW HOW TO

UN-MUFFLE THEM!"

Chapter Seven

The Show Goes On And Cyclone Purrs

It *was* time.

The audience *was* arriving!

Then the garden gate clicked

and Miss Wand appeared.

She was carrying an easel,

a basket of paints

and Cyclone in the basket!

She settled
near the fairies' stage
though not too near...
for she always knew not to look
too directly at fairies.

"Oh dear," Fingers peered out
between the curtains.
"They're all going to be
so disappointed,
with Rainbow, Speedwell,
Elfie and Bristle
not able to be heard!"

"And it's nearly all my fault,"
said Nogo, glaring over at Cyclone.
"But wait! I've had an idea!

"They can still do *something*.
Fingers, ask everyone to hold on
while Bristle and I fly home
for a few things. Come on, Bristle,
our concert must go on!"
And he and Bristle flew off
as fast as they could...

And when they got
back, that's just
what happened...
the concert went on!
Rainbow and Speedwell
    played Nogo's pot and pan drums.
            Elfie juggled his acorn
                cups. Bristle did a
                Magic Brush,
            Pan and Interesting
    Twig dance. And in between
these new acts,
the fairies who
weren't muffled
played their parts
beautifully.

When it was over,
the audience clapped
and cheered.
Miss Wand tapped
her brush on
her easel
and Fingers
invited
the whole
audience to the
After-Concert party.

Luckily, Speedwell had baked
enough for everyone.

"Delicious, Speedwell!" cried Nogo.

"Try one of your own Magic
Muffins. I've never tasted
anything so magic!"

"Nor me!" said Rainbow
with her mouth full.

"Rainbow!" cried Fingers.

"You spoke and we heard!
Here, Elfie, Bristle... quick,
eat one of these!"

"So that's the secret of undoing my
magic!" said Nogo amazed.
"Magic Muffins! I must
remember that.
And look what else
I remembered..."
He held up the other little sack
the Peaspods' had fished up.
"I'd like to give it to you, Rainbow."

Rainbow pulled the ivy cord
and peered inside.
At once her face shone
like a buttercup
and HER good manners
came rushing back.
"Oh, Nogo," she sighed.
"I've been so bossy today.
No wonder you muffled me!"

She bent down
and gave him the lightest kiss.
"Sorry. Truly sorry, Nogo...
all of you."
And, as no one had ever heard
Rainbow say sorry for anything,
they all clapped and cheered.

Miss Wand tapped her brush loudly,
while Cyclone did something
he never did near fairies...
He curled up in the paint basket
and purred!